Copyright © 2021 by Andy Slinger

First paperback edition April 2021

Book design by Andy Slinger
Illustrations by Kate Mottershaw

ISBN (paperback) 978-1-8381013-2-9
ISBN (ebook) 978-1-8381013-3-6
Published by Twin Dad Ltd
www.andyslinger.com

Dedication

This book is dedicated to my wonderful parents without whom I wouldn't have got where I am today. I may not say it enough, but I truly appreciate and love you. I also can't forget my amazing twin boys, Luke and Liam, who are my inspiration every single day.

Prologue

Since the defeat of the dark zombie army in the Battle of Wheatsheaf Hill, our heroes Ryan and Jake, the Super Twins and leaders of the Alliance of Superheroes, have become local celebrities. In gratitude for all they have done for the town of Trincaster, the local mayor has decreed a statue be erected in their honour.

The whole town will celebrate at the annual Trincaster Fast Food Festival, where the unveiling of the statue will take place. This will be the biggest celebration the town has seen since the notorious Mud Pie Carnival painted the town brown. There will be stalls, games… and loads of greasy food.

All the local residents are ridiculously excited at the prospect of the festivities. However, there is one person who will not be taking part. One person whose sole aim and objective is to destroy the fun.

This man, the Super Twins' father, changed beyond all recognition into his alter-ego, Evil Dad, when a ginormous meteorite destroyed their house and left the boys with their incredible Superpowers.

He's been in hiding since the infamous battle,

plotting his revenge and the destruction of the boys' statue. The thought of a festival filled with fun, excitement – and especially junk food –makes him want to puke.

During his time in the shadows, Evil Dad has become more and more evil. The green piece of meteorite which bejewels his staff has altered his mind beyond recognition.

Using this meteorite, a mysterious alien race known as the Auxen are controlling Evil Dad for their own purposes and they are intent on world domination…

Chapter One

"A great rise comes after a great fall. Let them enjoy their glory for the time being. When the time comes, they will realise that their moment of triumph meant nothing. The opportunity for the Super Twins to join with me and conquer the world has been and gone. Now's the time for the dark army to take control. You, Gedeon, will stand beside me as the Super Twins beg for mercy."

Evil Dad motioned to the side of him and Gedeon took his position in the chair to the right of his throne. "You've served me well, Gedeon, and your loyalty and willingness to do what is necessary will be rewarded. From here onwards, you will be general of my army and you'll carry out my wishes as commanded."

"My lord, thank you for this honour. I won't let you down. Your wish is my command. Together we'll destroy the Super Twins." Gedeon smiled a cruel and unwavering smile as his menacing eyes met Evil Dad's, but he couldn't hold his gaze for long.

The dark lord didn't flinch, his piercing glare sending a shudder down the newly appointed general's spine. "I trust you understand the plan? We must put a stop to all this fun and destroy this ridiculous Fast Food Festival. I will not fail a second time; any mistakes will be severely punished."

His leader still hadn't blinked as Gedeon bowed his head in submission. "Yes, I understand, my lord."

"Well then, what are you waiting for? There's much to be done. You must notify the army of your change in position and begin the preparations."

Evil Dad slammed his staff hard into the metallic floor, the green piece of meteorite on top of it glowing brightly. He watched his general jump to his feet, salute, and march out of the guarded door in front of him. *"Gedeon has the perfect qualities I need to lead this army,"* he thought. *"He's mean and vicious, with a cruel streak. He'll serve me well, or he'll feel the true force of dark energy that runs through my veins."*

Evil Dad was immediately interrupted by the voice of the Auxen, who had penetrated his mind: *"Don't get carried away without us. Remember who gave you your powers, Evil Dad. Don't forget we are relying on you to find the last ingredient for our formula, Mutagen E. This will transform our army into an unstoppable force. Once the army is ready, you must destroy this absurd festival and take over the town. When we have control of the town, we can destroy those pesky Super Twins forever and take on the world."*

The voices in his head wouldn't go away; they

kept taking over Evil Dad's mind. The Auxen had gifted him incredible powers through the meteorite in his staff and he owed them so much. He had to follow their orders and he would do exactly as they said. He'd change the world into a place with no trace of the past; a world of strong, hardworking people, where vegetables covered every plate. And if it took getting rid of the Super Twins to achieve it then so be it...

Chapter Two

Jake hurled the tomato sauce across the table a little harder than he had meant to. It bounced hard off Ryan's forehead before landing with a cushioned flump in the cloudlike mashed potato that sat in the middle of the antique dining table.

"Have you lost the ability to catch all of a sudden?" laughed Jake as he rocked back on his chair.

Ryan's glare said it all. He wasn't going to be goaded by his brother, not during Sunday lunch at least. In his mind he visualised the rows and rows of fine china accidentally falling off the shelving unit behind his brother and smashing onto his head. *"Ohh what a shame that would be,"* Ryan thought.

"Brussel sprouts anyone?" their tiny grandma enquired.

"Noooooo…" the boys yelled at exactly the same time.

"…thank you," added Ryan.

"No problem. It'll just mean more for me and the cats." The Super Twins' grandma chuckled as she laid the mammoth bowl of sprouts on the perfectly positioned table mat in front of her.

This created a puzzle in Ryan's mind: was the terrible stench in the night coming from Grandma's bottom or the cats'? Perhaps some things were better left unanswered.

Grandma finished laying the remainder of the Sunday feast on the table before taking her position at the head of it. "So, boys, what are your plans for this afternoon? I was thinking we could have a game of cards. I'll make us a big pot of tea and bake my special scones."

Ryan loved the idea of the scones as long as his grandma didn't mistake the cottage cheese for clotted cream again. That had been a very messy experience, especially when they realised that the cheese was a month out of date. The problem was, he always won at cards. His memory was so good he could memorise the whole deck in twenty seconds.

Besides, he and Jake couldn't hang around with Grandma – they needed to meet up with Jimmy and the gang. There were preparations for the Trincaster Fast Food Festival that needed to be completed. They had to make sure the event – and the unveiling of their statue – ran smoothly.

"We've sort of got plans this afternoon, Grandma," Ryan said. "I hope you don't mind."

"Have we?" chirped in Jake, with the usual empty expression on his face.

"Yes, we have…" replied Ryan, forcefully.

"We are meeting Jimmy and the others, remember?"

Jake stared blankly at his brother, completely unaware of the obvious hint. "Oh ok, we'd best eat up then, hadn't we, Ryan?!"

Ryan could tell that something wasn't quite right with Jake recently. He kept losing his temper and Ryan felt that his brother was becoming more distant from him every day. He'd tried to talk to him but he seemed grumpy, irritable and snappy. Since they had come to live with her, Grandma had been extremely patient with the two boys. Whatever they wanted she was more than happy to provide; nothing was too much trouble. It made Ryan feel warm inside that they had at least one family member that loved and cared about them.

"If you need to go, I understand, boys. Please just let me know if you'll be back for tea – it'll give me chance to get on with my jobs. There are plenty of cakes that need making for the celebrations and they won't make themselves. I have three tonnes of butter that could go to waste if I don't crack on!"

Grandma really was good to them, but Ryan wondered if she was trying to make up for the twins' not having their mum and dad around. Their lives had changed forever after the Battle of Wheatsheaf Hill.

But Ryan didn't have time to be thinking about

the past. He had to make sure the Alliance of Superheroes was ready for action, and the last thing he wanted was some bad guys trying to ruin their big day.

Evil Dad may have been defeated, but since the epic battle, things had gone quiet…

A little too quiet…

Chapter Three

"Out of my way, I know where I'm going. I need Laboratory 13." Gedeon barged past the meek scientists in their little white lab coats.

"But sir, Laboratory 13 is top level-access only. We've been told to not let anyone in that way," said one scientist.

"What do I look like to you, you snivelling little snowdrop? I'm the general of the army. Are you saying I can't have access when Evil Dad himself has ordered me to come here? Let me through, NOW!"

At once, the scientists cowered to one side of the corridor, letting the big brute of a man past.

That's more like it! This is what real power is all about," Gedeon thought.

Gedeon's sole aim was to get into the lab, find out which ingredients were required to complete the formula and obtain them by any means necessary. He had to be the one to take the glory, to demonstrate his capabilities to the Auxen. He needed to prove he was even more important than Evil Dad.

He had to be shown the respect he deserved. This wasn't about anyone else but him. Without him there wouldn't be an Evil Dad, without him there wouldn't be an army, and without him, those blasted Super Twins would have destroyed them all.

Evil Dad's general stomped down the corridor, pushing past anyone who got in his way. As he turned the corner, he was faced with a bronze-coloured plaque that read: '*Laboratory 13 – Top Secret*' above a set of shiny silver sliding doors. The doors were being protected by a pair of heavily armoured sentries.

"Open those doors now!" Gedeon growled at the men, who instantly stepped forwards, raising their weapons and pointing them right at him. "You are making a grave mistake, young protectors."

Gedeon sprang forwards, grabbing the end of one of their paint guns and whipping it round in an arc. The butt of the gun bounced off one guard's head, ricocheted onto the other and left them both in a heap on the floor. "I told you you were making a mistake," he sneered as he stepped over the second man, opened the door and inhaled deeply.

His eyes panned across a huge, white laboratory, where swarms of geeky-looking scientists were beavering away at their workstations. Test tubes, conical beakers full of fizzing, bubbling liquids, powders and solutions adorned their desks.

In the centre of the room stood a ginormous, domed glass chamber, with a door at the front. Huge swirling coils of metal came down from the ceiling and attached at the top of the structure. Electrical cabling ran through the right-hand side and ran along the floor, leading to a smaller dome made of thick metal. It contained all manner of switches, levers and dials.

Over on the left wall of the lab were rows of plastic cages full of animals: everything from badgers to moles and parrots to weasels. Gedeon strode forward, the *tip-tap* of his boots reverberating around the lab as he descended the metal stairs.

"Who's in charge here?" his voice boomed.

Everyone stopped dead at their workstations and turned to face the general. A small scientist wearing thick orange glasses on a bald head that was shining with grease scuttled across the room, clipboard in hand. "Can I be of assistance? I'm Professor Bios, and yes, I'm in charge here."

"You *were* in charge, Professor, but now I am in control. Evil Dad has sent me here to get this little project up to speed. Swiftly tell me your progress and what needs to be done to get to the next stage?"

"But... Evil Da…"

"But nothing," spat Gedeon. "I said swiftly."

"O… okay… t-t-t-trials have gone extremely w-w-w-well so far. We are close to having a fully active formula." Bios wiped away the sweat dripping from his brow.

"Close is not good enough. I want the formula ready now. There can be no delays!"

"B… B… But we are missing a vital ingredient – a substance called Mutagen E. We can't continue without it and there is no way of us getting it."

The Professor's head sank into his neck as he awaited the wrath of Gedeon, but the general looked at him and smiled. "You will get Mutagen E, mark my words, Bios…"

Chapter Four

As Ryan, Jake and Jimmy wandered into the Steamy Bag café, the little bell tinkled on the door as it swung shut.

Ryan headed straight over to the vending machine and typed in number 53. Jimmy stared at him in disbelief. "Why on earth would you chose those disgusting sweets?" he quizzed.

"Because nobody else ever will. Watch and learn, Jimmy; watch and learn."

The machine made a clunking noise. Ryan grabbed the metal handle of the vending machine and opened it up to reveal a stone staircase.

"Welcome to the brand-new Alliance of Superheroes Headquarters."

"What on earth…? Why didn't I know about this?" Jimmy cried, in shock.

The boys darted behind the machine and down the cold, damp stairway until they reached the heart of their brand-new base. Jimmy's jaw dropped in amazement as he scanned the room. It was full of all the latest technology: computers, surveillance-camera screens and in the centre of the room, a hi-tech interactive computer table.

Vortex, the former leader of the Alliance of

Superheroes, sat proudly at the table and smiled as the boys walked towards him. His long white beard betrayed his advancing years and his blue robes flowed over the arms of his chair. "I didn't recognise you there without your Superhero suit on, Gold Shield," he said to Jimmy. "If you pop into that room there, you'll find a shiny new outfit for you. But hurry, I'm not waiting – we have a meeting to get underway."

Jimmy quickly scampered off to grab his new gold-plated armour. He was soon sitting down at the table as Gold Shield, in between the Super Twins, with the biggest smile ever on his face.

Vortex began the meeting. "On the agenda today: the annual Fast Food Festival security measures; Professor Bios; cream cakes and any other business." Vortex stroked his beard as he spoke. "Who wants to start?"

The Alliance of Superheroes started by discussing the Fast Food Festival and who would be responsible for what on the day. Gold Shield would be responsible for weaponry and monitoring the security cameras. Vortex would provide personal security for the town mayor and the Super Twins at the unveiling.

As a matter of urgency, the Super Twins would work together to investigate some rumours that were circulating around Trincaster. According to a local takeaway delivery driver, there were murmurings of a mysterious dark force at the Trincaster army barracks. An ominous green glow had been spotted there at night and the twins were convinced it had something to do with the return of Evil Dad.

Jake was also highly suspicious of their old IT teacher, Professor Bios, who'd been spotted working in the lab after school. Jake had never trusted him, especially not after the huge explosion in the school kitchen last term. The boys would have to keep a close eye on the Professor. The last thing the Alliance wanted was the rise of an evil, fast food-hating force again so close to the festival.

"Now that we have a plan, does anyone have any other business?" Vortex asked.

"Yes, how about an opening for a brand-new member of the Alliance?" said Gold Shield.

Ryan swung around to see a girl with bright purple pigtails, luminous blue and orange stripy tights and bright white trainers standing in the doorway. Ryan jumped to his feet.

"Calm down, Ryan, it's ok," said Gold Shield as he pushed his thick rimmed spectacles up his nose. "I think you'd best come in and sit down." He gestured to the girl.

"How did you get in here? Do you know her, Jimmy... I mean, Gold Shield?" quizzed Ryan.

"Yes, this is my cousin, Laila," answered Gold Shield.

"I know all about her, I told her how to get in," Vortex added.

"But we're not recruiting anyone at the moment!" Ryan was furious that Alliance security was so relaxed as he watched the girl stride towards Jake.

"Budge up, you're taking up the place of two people there, Mr Happy," Laila teased Jake.

Jake didn't react well. "Maybe I don't want anyone sitting next to me, especially not a girl!" he retorted whilst extending his legs and arms out to fill the remaining space on the bench.

"You really shouldn't have said that," she responded, digging Jake in the ribs with her knuckles before swinging her leg over the bench and claiming her spot at the table. "You're Jake, right?" she said as she held out her hand to shake his.

"Yeah, and what's it to you?" Jake turned his body away from Laila, ignoring her outstretched hand. He gave his brother a look. This girl was going to be impossible to ignore and Jake got the feeling she wasn't going to leave him alone in a hurry.

"Can we please carry on with any other business?" Vortex raised his voice above the team. "All new recruits to the Alliance of Superheroes must first be voted in and second, they must pass an initiation test. Gold Shield and I have invited

Laila here, so she should be given a fair chance. All those in favour of Laila's induction make yourself known."

Gold Shield and Vortex both raised their hands, while Ryan stared across at his brother Jake who was looking down at the table.

"Looks like, with my vote, I'm in!" laughed Laila as she raised her arm. "So, what's the initiation test?"

Jake sighed in disbelief.

"I think she should be involved in the Bios mission," suggested Gold Shield. "As you are the one with the suspicions, she should go with you, Jake."

"Agreed," laughed Ryan, who found it hilarious that his twin had been dumped with the girl.

"Right, that's final," decided Vortex. "Jake and Laila will do some investigations into Bios while Ryan will investigate the army camp with me."

Jake looked over at his brother in despair. How had he been landed with the new recruit?

Chapter Five

One kick and the window smashed to smithereens. Evil Dad leaped through the gap and his size-ten boots crunched glass against the concrete floor.

Gedeon had provided him with all the information he needed to gain access to the Mutagen E. But if he thought he was leaving this task to him he was very much mistaken. Brute force was Gedeon's strong point, but he was severely lacking in stealth and finesse. Evil Dad would be in and out of the place in no time and then he could really kickstart his plan.

He crept down the corridor. The only noise came from his cloak which wafted out behind him, as he seamlessly floated along up a flight of metal stairs. He knew where he needed to be. He'd give himself less than five minutes before the alarm was sounded. As he approached the doorway into level 7, he heard chattering from two of the night guards:

"These night shifts are taking their toll; I may be earning a decent crust but I'm lucky if I catch more than five minutes a day with the kids," said one guard.

"I know what you mean. I find myself falling

asleep everywhere. The other day I was walking home and I fell asleep standing up! It was a good job I opened my eyes when I did – I nearly walked into that huge statue they're going to be unveiling in the town square." He laughed.

The Auxen knew what needed to be done and they wasted no time instructing Evil Dad: *"Destroy the guards. Don't leave anything to chance. Our plans cannot be compromised by your failure to finish the job again."*

"Yes, I'll do as you command. I serve only you and I won't fail you this time," replied Evil Dad.

"If you fail us again, it will be the end for you. Any connection you had to those troublesome twins is over. Now do as we instructed."

"Yes, masters, I won't let you down."

Evil Dad burst through the door and leaped through the air, a double kick ensuring the two guards were knocked out on the ground within a fraction of a second. With a swoosh of his powerful staff, he lifted the men off the ground and back out through the open door. There, he left them slumped in the corner, dribbling on each other.

Now he was really going to have to move quickly. It was only a matter of time before the alarm would be sounded and he still had to get out of there.

He charged down the corridor, firing a burst of

power from his staff which ripped the solid-steel door straight off its hinges. Dashing through the doorway he quickly scanned the room. There were rows and rows of metal racking stretching as far as the eye could see, all the way up to the extremely high ceiling. On each shelf he could see barrel after barrel of chemicals, all marked up with the contents clearly visible on the outside.

But there was no Mutagen E. Where on earth was it?

Evil Dad sprinted up and down the aisles, dragging barrels off the top shelves using the power of his mind. The Mutagen E had to be in here somewhere.

He searched row after row and was beginning to lose hope, when out of the corner of his eye he spotted a door hidden in the corner. A large skull-and-crossbones symbol with the word TOXIC written below it told him this might be exactly what he was looking for.

Suddenly, alarm sirens began to wail, half-deafening Evil Dad as he stomped through the doorway. His eyes lit up at a huge haul of containers, all clearly marked with the TOXIC symbol and the words Mutagen E. This was what he had come for.

Zaaapppp!

The back wall of the building crumbled with a tiny flourish of his staff. Evil Dad's cloak began to flap wildly as a strong gust of wind burst into the room, the remaining walls jangling and groaning while he pushed forwards. The noise was deafening.

Using his mind, he lifted a huge barrel of Mutagen E, ran for the edge of the building and leaped into the air. Then with one hand, he grabbed onto a rope ladder that was dangling from a helicopter above.

Chapter Six

Cups and saucers tinkled, whilst crumbs bounced onto the freshly laid tablecloth. The gentle babble of voices young and old filled the air, over the crackle of the local radio station.

The Alliance of Superheroes was crowded around a little table in the centre of the Steamy Bag café, elbows banging into one another as they scoffed down scones with clotted cream and jam.

"Whose idea was it to come in here? We're never out of this place," teased Ryan as he gulped down a cup of piping-hot tea in one swig.

"Have you no feeling in your throat or something?" jibed his brother. "That tea is hot enough to kill any taste buds you have left."

"You're acting like you don't get fed or watered at home with the number of cups of tea you've downed in the last five minutes," Laila chuckled. Ryan slowly and deliberately lowered his cup down to the little round saucer in front of him, looking embarrassed.

Laila whispered something in Jake's ear. He responded with a chuckle. It made Ryan sick to look at them. They'd been given one mission together and suddenly they were best friends. Ryan hadn't even spoken to his brother in the past week and time was running out before the festival. They hadn't even started investigating Professor Bios.

At least Jimmy had his back and cared about the Superhero Alliance. They could plan the security for the festival and investigate Bios and the army camp without Jake and probably do a better job of it. He didn't need his twin anyway. He was careless at the best of times and what the Alliance needed now was careful planning and his brains.

"Hey, Jake, your girl has something stuck on her chin!" Ryan belly laughed but the pair didn't seem to see the funny side of it. Laila shot up out of her chair, heading straight to the bathroom to check herself out. A chunk of scone swung from her jaw, attached to a stringy piece of jam.

As she stormed past Ryan, she shot him a glare. She proceeded to swipe the back leg of his chair with her foot so hard, it shot off like an ice hockey puck under a nearby table. The result was catastrophic for Ryan – his chair rocked, wiggled and jiggled, and his arms flailed around in mid-air before he came crashing down on the floor. He lay there winded, staring up at the yellowing ceiling, while everyone in the café erupted in laughter.

A young waitress scurried over and scrambled to help him up off the floor. Embarrassed didn't even come close to how he felt at that moment.

The girl pulled over another chair and helped Ryan sit down before topping up his teacup with a little smirk. Ryan tried to avoid eye contact with everyone around him, especially the jubilant Laila as she returned to the table. She'd gone too far. If she'd wanted to wind him up, she'd succeeded.

"We interrupt this broadcast to bring you breaking news. This morning at approximately 3:00 am, there was a break-in at the Nimor chemical plant, on the Trincaster Industrial Estate. Two guards were badly injured but are currently stable in hospital. A spokesperson from the plant said: 'Whoever is responsible for this knew exactly what they were looking for. The stolen chemical, Mutagen E, has been known to turn humans into mutant animals.'"

Ryan jumped up out of his chair. "Come on, Jimmy, we need to get out of here!"

"But wait, slow down, where are you going?" stuttered Jake.

Ryan spoke in a hushed voice: "We've got work to do. If I'm right, I know exactly who is behind this and it starts with an E and ends in a D. If he's building a mutant army like I think he is then we need a weapon to counteract it. Jimmy and I need to make a start on it right now – we have no time to waste. Besides, you guys need to go after Bios."

Jake groaned. He wished he'd never mentioned the Professor now. He hated how his brother was always right.

Chapter Seven

"Begin the testing!"

Evil Dad ushered the men to their positions around Laboratory 13. Now was the moment he'd been waiting for. All the elements were in place. In just a few moments his evil army would become an unstoppable force.

He would do as the Auxen had commanded, sending his army into the town square and taking control of the unveiling ceremony. If the Alliance of Superheroes got in the way, he would use Gedeon to destroy the Super Twins once and for all.

His eyes fixated upon the wolf inside the large glass dome, which was running around in circles chasing its tail. As the chamber began to fill with green smoke, the animal disappeared from view completely.

"Now!" commanded Gedeon, who was standing beside Evil Dad, but no one moved a muscle. "Come on, what are you waiting for, you fools?!"

"Patience, my friend. Observe history in the making. This is something that's never been done before. With the power the Auxen have given me, I can begin shaping the world as I've always dreamed."

With that, Evil Dad raised his staff and drove it down into the ground. A lightning bolt shot out from the meteorite across the room, fizzing as it hit the cabling on the side of the dome.

The room juddered and the scientists held onto anything within their reach. A deafening drone emanated from the electrical shock wave. The scientists scrambled to cover their ears whilst others dived down onto the ground. Evil Dad held his arms aloft as the power flowed through his entire body, his focus entirely upon the dome.

Suddenly, silhouetted by the green glow of the chamber, stood Gedeon. He'd jumped in the middle of the experiment and was staring straight back at the dark lord, his eyes wild. A disturbing evil grin spread across his face as he laughed hysterically, the electricity consuming him. His body began to vibrate as he roared and fell to his knees.

Crash!

Behind him, the glass shattered as the green gas enveloped him and Evil Dad lowered his staff.

The laboratory was plunged into silence and smoke filled the air. Several lab technicians tentatively rose to their feet, cautiously moving to the back of the room. Gradually, the smog began to disperse and the sight which met Evil Dad's eyes was something unimaginable. The wolf had completely vanished and there, crouched on all fours staring back at him, was Gedeon. But he was not as he had been seen before.

As he rose to his feet it became apparent he had transformed into something which could no longer be considered human. His face was partially covered in hair, his jaws extended forwards and razor-sharp teeth protruded over his lips. His shirt had been burnt from his back and revealed a body two or three times the size of a regular man. Every muscle fibre in his chest was visible, his hands were huge, with jagged claws protruding from the end of his fingers.

The voice of the Auxens echoed in Evil Dad's mind: *"He must be ours to control. We must use him to our advantage."*

Gedeon stepped forward, the terrifying beast of a man looking straight at Evil Dad before he bowed and knelt down on one knee. "I am yours to command, master," he growled.

Chapter Eight

Meanwhile, in the Alliance Headquarters below the Steamy Bag café…

"You know what this means, don't you?" said Ryan.

"What's that?" enquired Jimmy.

"It's what I've been saying all along. If I'm right, and most of the time I am, Evil Dad is back. That, along with the threat of Bios and the mysterious disappearance of Mutagen E, is not the news we needed. It's bad enough that Evil Dad has returned, he sucks the fun out of everything. But if he's planning to build a mutant army like I think he is, then it could spell catastrophe for Trincaster.

"We know he'll target the Fast Food Festival – the last thing he'll want is to see the town celebrating our success with burgers, pizzas and chicken nuggets. And then, to see a statue of the Super Twins unveiled on top of all that will send him crazy. There is no way he will resist trying to stop the celebrations."

"But how do you know all this?" questioned Jimmy.

"That meteorite gave me super-intelligence Jimmy, you know that. But it not only affected me and Jake, it also affected Evil Dad. I've been thinking about this for a long time: I strongly believe something from outer space is controlling him through it. They have to be, I know there is still good in him somewhere. But if he's being controlled by some alien species and has a mutant army as well, then we're in very real danger. I need you to put all your focus into creating a weapon that will disable these mutants. If you can manage that, then we might just stand a chance."

Ryan wandered over to the mass of computer screens and began to scroll through the video images they had taken from around the town. Nothing seemed amiss, people were going about their day-to-day business as usual, without a care in the world.

Since the Battle of Wheatsheaf Hill, the general population of Trincaster seemed happier than ever. Ryan watched a small boy run and jump up on his dad's leg, scaling him like a climbing frame, before his dad swung the lad around his head and plonked him on his shoulders. The young boy laughed and squealed with joy. Ryan clicked to move onto the next camera image.

"We have to act swiftly and decisively here. No messing around, no mercy. We have to mobilise everyone we've got and stop whatever is going on before something really bad happens." Ryan slammed his hand down on the desk as he spoke.

"But Ryan, you don't actually know what's

going on though, do you? You're guessing."
Vortex appeared from the shadows and limped
over towards the twin, supported by a walking
stick. "It's ok saying we need to act quickly and
decisively, but who or what are you acting
decisively against? Evil Dad might be back, but you
don't know where he is hiding. If you want my
opinion then we sit tight, increase patrols, study
the cameras, and get to the root of what's going
on. The last thing this town needs right now is a
maverick Super Twin taking on an invisible force
by himself!" Vortex stroked his long, white beard
as he spoke with the assurance and calm that came
with his advanced years.

"I'm the leader of this Alliance," retaliated
Ryan. "If I say we need to act, then we need to act.
I can't just sit back and let him destroy the festival
everyone has worked so hard on!"

"What about Jake?" chimed in Gold Shield.
"You don't have to do this without him."

"What about him? He's busy tracking Bios
with Laila. I'm here now and we need to act. I
don't always need my twin to do everything with
me."

Ryan turned back towards the screens to
contemplate his next move. Why did everyone
always assume he couldn't cope without his
brother? It was starting to irritate him. He'd reveal
Evil Dad was behind the robbery of the Nimor

chemical plant all by himself. Well, with the help of Gold Shield – at least he could be relied on.

Why have two Super Twins when the world only needed one? Together with Jimmy, he'd create a formula to destroy the mutants in no time and take the glory. He continued to bash the computer control panel as Jimmy came to stand next to him.

"It's ok, you know. I'm here for you, mate. Whatever you decide to do I'll be by your side." Jimmy, in his full gold armour, gave him a friendly jab to the ribs, something that only he could get away with.

"Wait! Go back to the previous screen. No, not that one, the one before. There, look!" Jimmy was jumping up and down and pointing excitedly.

"What, what is it?" Vortex hobbled over, intrigued.

"There in the top left of the image. Can you see that?" he was frantic now. "Come on, zoom in, quickly!"

Ryan zoomed in as far as he could and there, as clear as day, was an army jeep being loaded with barrels of TOXIC Mutagen E. They watched as a group of soldiers pulled a tarpaulin over the top of the barrels and sped off.

"I knew it!" yelled Ryan. "Not only is Evil Dad back, but now we know he's at the army base!"

Chapter Nine

"Where are we going? Don't just stomp off like that – you need to let me know what's going on!" Laila struggled to keep up with Jake as he stormed down the road.

"You'll know soon enough. Now keep up, I'm not being slowed down by you."

He didn't have time to wait for her. If he was going to be stuck with her, he was going to do things his way, at his pace. Jake knew that Bios was up to no good, he just had to prove it to the others. He was disappointed that his brother had palmed him off like that, now he wanted to get this mission over and get back to the Alliance as quickly as possible.

"Hey, are we nearly there yet? This is getting ridiculous!" Laila didn't look impressed.

Jake felt it wise to slow down the pace slightly. "Yeah, don't worry, it's just around the next corner." He didn't want to stop now.

"Are you sure? Listen, Jake, just stop a second. I want to tell you something." She grabbed his arm and gave him a cheeky little smile that set his cheeks on fire.

He turned away and saw a powerfully built milkman decorating his milk van with garlands of pink flowers ready for the festival. He looked at the ground.

"I know you think the others are doubting you, but I wanted you to know I've got faith in you."

"Is that it?" Jake said, baffled. "Come on, I don't have time for this."

He led Laila right to the edge of Trincaster town centre, over a fence and through a field laden with cow muck and boggy marshland. Their feet squelched as they made steady progress through the filth. Laila nearly lost a trainer on a couple of occasions and relied on Jake yanking her out of the mud with his powerful grip.

Before long, they reached a more hospitable field, but they still faced pieces of broken machinery and tractor tyres.

"Right, this is it. Hurry up, be quick!" Jake called urgently as he disappeared under a big blue sheet and out of sight.

They were back at the original Alliance of Superheroes base, which hadn't been used since Ryan, in his great wisdom, had decided to transfer all their stuff to the new café headquarters.

"So, what do you think of it?" asked Jake.

"What do I think of what?" replied Laila in the most unenthusiastic way possible. "This place is a complete dump! Why on earth have you brought me here? We'd have been better off sitting in that field amongst the cow poo!"

"Now, now, come on, it's not that bad. This was our first Alliance base. We haven't used it for months, so it needs a bit of a spring clean. Anyway, you haven't seen anything yet. Come through here and check out the armoury."

Jake led Laila under the blue sheet into a dark space. Using his voice to activate the controls, the place grumbled, groaned then sprang into life. Walls rotated round and secret cabinets opened to reveal lots of empty shelves.

"Well, it's hardly the haul of weapons you'd expect in an armoury, Jake. I think I'll be better off with my bare hands if we end up facing any action!" She kicked a stray tin of beans that ricocheted off the wall and landed in front of him.

"Hahaha, you'll need any weapons you can get your hands on with a kick like that!"

"Put your money where your mouth is, Super Twin." Laila grimaced as she raised her hands up in a fighting stance. "You'll live to regret saying that."

She lunged forward at incredible speed, flipped once, twice, turned and cartwheeled towards Jake. In an instant she landed down in a crouched position, spun around and swept Jake's legs from under him with a low kick.

The next thing he knew he was laid out flat on his back, staring up at a cobweb on the ceiling, with Laila's stinking, sludge-covered foot pushed up against his neck.

"Okay I get the message Laila, you win. I think we should grab these smoke and paint bombs and head to the school," said Jake. "I want to find out exactly what Bios is up to."

***

Jake and Laila crouched down behind the stone wall. There were no signs of movement. Maybe he was wrong about Bios after all, and maybe Evil Dad was behind the chemical plant robbery.

"Have you spotted anything yet?" he asked Laila.

"Not a single thing," she replied with a sigh. "We should get out of here, it's getting dark. People will wonder where we are."

"Wait… Not so soon," whispered Jake.

Over in the chemistry labs there was a flicker of torchlight.

"That's got to be him." Jake was getting excited. He was going to prove his brother wrong for once. "I reckon he's concocting his experiments in there. I knew we couldn't trust him!"

Jake's ears pricked up as he heard a rumble down at the far end of the dirt track behind the school. The rumble quickly became the roar of an engine as it approached the back entrance.

"It's an army jeep," muttered Laila.

"And look over there – coming from the back of the school. It's Bios…" growled Jake. "I knew it!" He ground his teeth as Bios jumped in the vehicle and sped off.

Chapter Ten

"What on earth were you playing at? You knew the plan and deliberately decided to go against my wishes. This is not the behaviour befitting of the general of my army! Lock him away."

Evil Dad signalled to the guards to approach Gedeon. They inched forward cautiously, their electric-shock guns pointed at the beast.

"Come on! What are you waiting for? He's nothing but a freak of nature now." Evil Dad couldn't believe the stupidity of the man for throwing himself in the middle of his mutant experiment like that – he could have been killed. He would have to lead this attack by himself; he couldn't rely on Gedeon for anything.

"But master, wait! Have faith in me! I'm exactly what you need now. I have the power to strike fear into the enemy. I can lead our dark forces into battle. I'm capable of capturing the Super Twins single-handedly and bringing them to you. I'm yours to command, I serve only you. I did this to give you the ultimate power. I did it all for you!" Gedeon was begging on his hands and knees.

"*Yes, he does have a point,*" thought Evil Dad. Gedeon was stupid to throw himself into the experiment like that, but the Auxen wanted to use the beast to their advantage. The wolfman could help him to change the world into what it should be: a planet of hardworking, vegetable-eating, organised and compliant individuals.

Under his leadership, this country, and in turn the world, would become a better place. But first he needed to gain complete control of Trincaster. Maybe, if he was clever, Gedeon could form a part of that plan. A wry smile formed as an image of the world bowing down to him filled Evil Dad's mind.

"I hope you aren't forgetting about us, Evil Dad. You know you would be powerless without us. Gedeon can, and will, lead our army. You will make him follow our orders. When the earth falls, you will kneel before the mighty Auxen and you will serve us."

"Yes, I will, master."

Evil Dad knew it was pointless to resist – the Auxen had the power to destroy him at any moment. He had to obey them, his life depended on it. He would tread cautiously and deal with the aliens later. His priority was building his vicious mutant army.

The experiment had worked. The capability was there to produce many more mutants, but time was running out. He had to act quickly to catch the Super Twins by surprise.

"Gedeon, arise, come with me. Now's the time for us to attack. Bios, start the next wave of production. I want an army ready and waiting by the end of the day!"

"Yes, sir – as you wish!"

Professor Bios bowed to Evil Dad and scampered off to begin work.

Chapter Eleven

The next day after school, Ryan stood outside the gates waiting for the rest of the crew to trundle out of the stone-clad building. He could never understand why someone with Super Speed was always the last one out of school at the end of the day.

Surely part of being thirteen was pretending you hated being at school, even if you didn't. It hardly made him a candidate for Cool Kid of the Year, hanging around, leaning against the fence. People might think he was waiting for a teacher or something. Ryan shivered at the thought.

After what felt like an age, Jake appeared out of the main entrance, laughing and joking with Laila. They were practically joined at the hip after their little adventure together. The closer they got to him, the more anxious Ryan felt. He had to tell them all about his discovery. "Hey, how's it going? You guys ok?" Ryan spoke as calmly as he could.

"You didn't need to wait for us. I thought you'd have more important things to do; things that I'm not involved with anymore." Jake looked at Laila as he spoke. "Anyway, we've discovered what's going on and it's down to Professor Bios. But you'd know that already, Mr Super Brain."

"That's no way to speak to me. We're a team — we do this together, remember? What happened with Bios?"

"We caught him sniffing around the chemistry block and then he sped off in an army vehicle."

"This is even more serious than we all thought, Jake. Evil Dad is definitely back and we've linked him with the army base too. He must be working with Bios. I'm convinced they're targeting the Fast Food Festival. We need to call an emergency Alliance meeting with the Trincaster mayor. He needs to know what's going on."

"Well, that's really nice of you to let me know about Evil Dad — I thought I'd be the first person you'd tell about that. You go and call your little meeting without me. I'm going to do what we should be doing together, and finish Evil Dad myself. This fame is going to your head. Come on, Laila, let's get out of here."

"Having an attitude like that is exactly why I've carried on doing the important things without you. And I told you about Evil Dad at the café — you just weren't listening! You need to remember we're an Alliance. It's not all about you and little Miss Princess here."

"She is called Laila," Laila spat. "And *she* knows everything there is to know about you guys and your little Super Twin adventures, so I'd be careful how you speak to me!"

"Are you threatening me? You're the problem here! Everything was just fine until you showed up, sticking your nose into everything. The Alliance was alright without you!" Ryan was getting redder and redder and louder and louder as he spoke.

"Right, that's enough, Ryan. Laila's done nothing wrong other than try to help us. You should be grateful. All that seems to concern you is your precious little Alliance, not the feelings of your identical twin. I think it's you that needs to consider what is important to you. Come on let's get out of here!" Jake stared at him right in the eye and stormed away.

Ryan stood there feeling hollow, alone and scared about what the future may hold. His brother had held no punches, and he'd said things he didn't mean as well.

Now he was going to have to meet with the mayor without Jake. The Super Twins as he knew them were no more…

Chapter Twelve

Evil Dad watched as the beast's muscles tensed in anticipation. His eyes moved at a stupendous speed, surveying the town hall from the edge of the cliff face, a mile away.

"The stench of the Alliance is filling my nostrils from here. I will show no mercy. They'll soon be at my whim and then we can take control of the town as you wish."

Gedeon snarled.

"Patience, Gedeon. I know you are eager to attack but we must wait for the right opportunity. Soon the Alliance will be getting ready to leave the town hall, completely unaware of our presence. When their guard is low, we can pounce."

As Evil Dad spoke, he listened into his general's mind:

"He really doesn't know what I'm capable of. I will take on the Alliance single-handedly and destroy those meddlesome twins. Then I will destroy Evil Dad and become leader of the dark army."

Evil Dad's voiced rasped out at him: "I can hear what you are thinking, Gedeon – you forget my powers. Don't think for one second that you will get one over on me! You may now have abilities that far exceed anything you thought humanly possible, but remember, without the Auxen and I, you would have nothing. You are here to serve us. Don't ever forget that!''

There was movement in the town hall's main entrance. Gedeon's eyes immediately focussed on the building. Trincaster's town mayor, sporting the official gold chain around his neck, left the building with two other men. The Alliance meeting must have finished, thought Evil Dad. It was time to move.

Gedeon began to growl as he awaited the order.

"Now, Gedeon. Go! Go! Go!"

The mutant drove his back legs hard into the ground, leaping off the edge of the cliff before bouncing up off the hard surface that met his paws. Gedeon's eyes were transfixed on the front door of the building as he bounded along at breakneck speed. A handful of passers-by ran off screaming, petrified at the sight of the wolfman speeding down the street. A man-mountain of a body builder squealed and fainted with shock as Gedeon just missed clashing into him.

The wolfman was getting closer and closer, with the town hall just a few hundred metres away. The door swung open and standing there with a look of total shock on his face was Ryan. The boy did a double-take and jumped back inside, slamming the huge oak door behind him.

Gedeon was still running full pelt as he crashed into the solid door. An almighty crunching sound resonated around the town as the wood splintered and split. He drove his claws into the wood, tearing and ripping chunks of timber away, his razor-sharp teeth snapping and gnashing in a frenzy. Bit by bit, the hole in the door was growing bigger. Nothing would stop him getting through.

Ryan, Gold Shield and Vortex were now visible. They had quickly gathered some makeshift weapons and were standing to the rear of the entrance hall, poised for battle.

"Stop right there or you'll be sorry!" yelled Ryan.

Three more swipes of his incredibly powerful claws and the door crumbled before Gedeon. He marched into the reception area, his hair standing on end. His eyes burned like lumps of coal from the fires of hell. He strode forwards with intention.

The three Superheroes side-stepped around the edge of the circular hall. Gedeon meant business, the Alliance members were now in great danger.

Chapter Thirteen

"Who are you? What are you? What are you doing here?" demanded Vortex, as he backed up against the marble wall of the town hall entrance.

"I'm your worst nightmare!" growled Gedeon. "And I'm here to destroy you!"

"Get back!" yelled Gold Shield, waving his new prototype weapon – which was a giant burger attached to the end of a baguette. "You've burst through the wrong door today!"

"Ohhh, you think so, do you? Hahaha! You think you're going to defend yourself with that?! I was going to eat you up, but it looks like I'm going to have to devour your measly weapon first!"

Gedeon lunged forwards, fangs bared, growling and swiping his claws. Vortex reacted immediately, leaping up over the top of him. Gold Shield dodged the wolfman and rolled off to the side while Ryan charged straight at him.

The Super Twin roared as he flew towards the beast, bashing him straight on the snout. Maybe this was going to be easier than he first thought.

Gedeon spun around, lashing out, sending Gold Shield careering into Vortex, who in turn smashed against one of the huge marble columns.

The wolfman dashed towards Ryan, butting him like a deranged bull and propelled him over to the other side of the room. This was more like the fight he expected. The mutant turned and charged back over towards Gold Shield, grabbing his cape with his teeth and spinning him wildly around his head before hurling him out of the front door.

Gold Shield wasn't going to wait around to see what was going to happen to him – he scrambled to his feet and sprinted off down the street.

By this point, Vortex was advancing fast towards Gedeon. He was spinning around at high speed, twirling his two hammers as he rotated.

Gedeon took a couple of hard blows to the head which sent the wolfman skidding backwards, scrambling for grip.

Ryan emerged from the side, smashing a doner kebab into his back legs. The stench as the fast food hit the wolfman's fur was unbearable and sent him into a frenzy. Gedeon flailed wildly at the pair of Alliance members, catching Vortex with his paw and scratching his face, leaving three red lines across his cheek.

"I'm getting out of here!" screamed Vortex as he scampered out of the front door, leaving Ryan to fight against the beast alone.

"Ohh look who's left – my favourite Super Twin." The mutant growled with contempt at the boy. "Not got your little brother here to back you up? I thought that you went everywhere together. It's no challenge to me facing just one of you!"

"I don't need him here to take you on, you foul beast!" Ryan cried.

"You'll wish you hadn't said that, Super Twin!" Gedeon yelled as he leaped forwards, his fearsome teeth bared menacingly.

They began to brawl with each other, Ryan hurling all manner of objects at the beast: a hat stand, an ornate clock and various sizes of official town-council umbrellas. Gedeon made light work of them all, ripping them to pieces with his razor-sharp teeth.

Ryan ducked and dived before disappearing through a small doorway and down a corridor. Gedeon sprinted after him in hot pursuit, his humongous shoulders taking half of the door frame with him in the process.

Ryan sprinted hard down a passageway, but Gedeon was gaining on him fast as Ryan quickly took a sharp right in front of him. The wolfman approached the turn at speed and drifted around the corner like a tank sliding across an ice-skating arena.

Ryan ran down the centre of a large changing room; rows and rows of lockers ran down either side of the space which had benches and a couple of water fountains running down its centre. He darted down to the rear of the room and into the shower block, where he peered out from inside a cubicle. Ryan watched as Gedeon paced down the locker room, pausing momentarily to smash open numerous locker doors.

As Gedeon trod closer and closer towards him, Ryan sensed his opportunity.

BAM, BAM, BAM, BAM!

He fired butter bombs, which ricocheted off the lockers all around the beast and splattered everywhere. His matted fur was instantly stuck together like glue. The mutant swivelled around, slipping and sliding on the layer of grease and Ryan was suddenly face to face with him.

The twin laughed heartily and pointed his fat gun right at Gedeon. He'd found his weakness. "Had enough yet, growler?"

This pushed the wolfman over the edge. He charged towards the boy like a bull who'd seen the reddest of red flags waved in front of him. The water fountain toppled over, sending a gigantic spray of water up into the air, flooding the room. Gedeon ripped the gun out of the boy's hand and whizzed the Super Twin over his head. Ryan bounced off the lockers and landed in a heap on the floor.

Gedeon stood over Ryan as he lay in a pool of buttery water, unable to move. "Now I'll finish you once and for all," he snarled as he raised his powerful arm, ready to deliver the final blow. He swung down hard and fast but suddenly yelped out in pain. The wolfman began to float up into the air.

"Arggghhh!" Gedeon cried out. His body twisted up and around in the air, a green glow circulating around his shape.

Ryan looked up to see the imposing figure of Evil Dad holding the wolfman in the air. "That's enough, Gedeon, your work here is done. I want him left alive, let's get out of here!"

Chapter Fourteen

"Jake, Jake, are you there? Talk to me… It's urgent. Ryan's been hurt!"

Jake could barely decipher the words through the terrible phone signal. "Hello? Jimmy? What do you mean he's been hurt? What's happened?" He shot a concerned look across at Laila. This sounded really serious. What on earth had his brother been up to now?

"We were just leaving HQ after the emergency meeting when this horrific beast attacked us, I had to get out – it was going to kill us all!" Jimmy's voice trembled as he spoke.

"Beast? What on earth are you talking about? What about Ryan?"

"He's badly hurt, Jake, I'm not going to lie. It was horrible, it was so big… so powerful: half-man, half-wolf. It was like nothing I've ever seen before. Vortex and I managed to get out, but Ryan fought on alone. He's ok, though – stable but confused. Vortex has quit completely."

"So where on earth did this thing come from? Come on, Jimmy, what do you know?" Jake demanded.

"I'm sorry to tell you, but it's Evil Dad. He's

back."

"Tell me something I don't know already, Jimmy." You're wasting my time here.

"We think he's hiding out in the army barracks. Before the meeting with the mayor, we saw an army truck transporting Mutagen E barrels. It's got to be connected."

Beeep!

Jake put down the phone. He already knew everything he needed to know. Why had his brother tried to take on the mutant himself? Ryan was lucky he wasn't too badly hurt – at least Gold Shield and Vortex had the good sense to get out of there.

Now it was down to him to stop Evil Dad destroying the Fast Food Festival. He didn't need a super brain like Ryan's to use his fists. He'd stop the villain before he attacked and take the glory for himself.

"Come with me, Laila. We're going to have to rush to the army barracks – the Alliance has been attacked, Ryan is injured and as I expected, it's up to us sort this out. Trincaster is depending on us…"

Chapter Fifteen

"How on earth could you be so stupid? Do you realise what you've done? The whole point of this mission was to take control of Trincaster, stop this wretched festival and the unveiling of the ridiculous statue. It was not to kill one of the Super Twins and make him a hero. You imbecile – have you the brain of an animal as well as the looks of one? It's a good job I stopped you before you went too far!" Evil Dad was furious. He slammed his hands down hard on the desk, sending a peanut shooting into the wolfman's eye.

"But sire, I... I had him!" Gedeon growled as he spoke and rubbed his now bright-red, half-closed eye.

"SILENCE! You were under strict instructions to obey my command. You went completely against my will, and now not only have we missed a valuable opportunity, you have alerted the whole of the town to our presence. You know what this means don't you? Every wannabe Superhero this side of Wheatsheaf is going to be looking out for us! You don't have the brains you were born with."

As he shouted, Evil Dad rose out of his chair and moved over towards the great glass window that was the main feature of his impressive office at the army barracks. He looked out at the mass of vehicles and soldiers as they ran around preparing the base for an assault. They wouldn't have long – if he knew Jake like he thought he did, he'd be on his way right now. He should be planning the attack on the Fast Food Festival and not dealing with this fool.

"Do you even understand what you've done? What's your problem?" Evil Dad yelled as he spotted a flicker of light in of the corner of his eye. "Gedeon!"

Evil Dad swung around and discovered the half-man, half-wolf creature creeping up behind him.

Zapppppp!

Evil Dad thrust his staff forwards, catapulting the grizzly Gedeon backwards with a shock wave from his meteorite. The wolfman yelped in pain as Evil Dad began infiltrating his mind:

"What makes you think you can trick me that easily, general? Did you honestly think you could jump me from behind and take my role as leader?"

"I wasn't, sir… I promise… I was just coming to see the progress of the troops, sir."

"You are treading on very thin ice and I will not tolerate any more of this behaviour. Try any more tricks like that and you'll be the first to be destroyed! You're becoming a liability, Gedeon. I expected much better of you."

Gedeon lowered himself down into the seat positioned on the other side of Evil Dad's desk. He gripped the arms of the red chair so tightly that his claws punctured the leather. He was trying to conceal his fangs but he couldn't help but bare them. His bulging eyes gave away the hatred the wolfman clearly had for his master.

Evil Dad needed to get this beast under control. He had to use him to destroy the precious statue at the festival and stop the Super Twins' moment of glory. He was mindful that one false move, or lapse in concentration, and Gedeon would jump at the opportunity to double-cross him. He'd have to keep a very close eye on him.

"This is your final warning. Go to the lab and see Bios. He has a small battalion ready for you to command. Take these troops and ensure they're armed and ready. Tonight, you're going to set a trap that will bring the curtain down at the finale of the Trincaster Fast Food Festival, something that no one will expect, especially not those troublesome twins. Now go and do as instructed. Once everyone is in position, await my command!"

Evil Dad was sure he detected a smirk on his face as Gedeon rose and marched towards the door.

"Yes, master."

Chapter Sixteen

"Ryan, Ryan, can you hear me?" Jimmy prodded him as he whispered in his ear.

It was hopeless. Ryan lay unconscious in the pool of buttery water, motionless, and with an expression that said he wasn't amused.

It had been at least twenty minutes since Gedeon and Evil Dad had fled the scene and five minutes since Jimmy had tiptoed tentatively back in. The guilt Jimmy felt was immense; if he hadn't run away and tried to save his own skin then maybe Ryan wouldn't be in this state.

The upended water fountain was still pumping out gallons of water at a mammoth rate – it was lucky that Ryan hadn't drowned in the sea of devastation, thought Jimmy. His temperature was dropping and he'd turned very pale. Jimmy had to get him out of there fast, but where could he take him? It wasn't like they could just rock up at the hospital and say:

"Hey, nursey, I've brought you a half-drowned Super Twin. Do you mind just bringing him back to life and we'll be back on our way? Oh, and please don't reveal his identity to anyone – we've got a crazy wolfman to defeat before we head back to school tomorrow."

His options were limited and Jimmy had little

or no knowledge of first aid. The lesson he'd had in school mostly consisted of bandaging George Creasley's arm. He'd wrapped it so tightly that the boy lost all feeling in his fingers before they turned bright purple. If it hadn't been for Miss Buxton's long nails and special ability to untie a triple knot with ease, then Creasley may have been taken to hospital. Jimmy had secretly hoped it would happen.

Anyway, his bandaging skills were of no use at that moment – a life raft and a pair of rubber arm bands would be much more valuable. He needed to think fast. Who could help him? And more to the point, who could help him and not ask too many questions? That was the real challenge.

And then he got it: the twins' Grandma. She was perfect! She was so old she wouldn't have a clue what was going on. He pulled Ryan's phone out of his pocket and dialled his home number.

***

The car screeched round the corner, black smoke billowing from its tyres. The windows on the vintage car rattled as heavy-metal music blared from the stereo. The vehicle mounted the kerbside before juddering to a stop as the door flung open. Out stepped Grandma sporting aviator shades, a leather jacket and ripped jeans. "Where is he?" she

yelled. "Get him in the back of here, now! We need to get him the heck out of here!"

In shock, Jimmy ran and grabbed the knocked-out Super Twin and dragged him to the car. He bundled him into the back seat and then jumped into the front. Before he could even close the passenger door, Grandma's foot had pushed the pedal to the metal and they'd set off at an alarming speed. Jimmy scrambled to get his seat belt on and clung to his seat for dear life.

The old lady had absolutely no fear. She drove through red lights, skidded around corners and found great delight in driving on the wrong side of the road. Jimmy covered his eyes and cowered as Grandma attempted to play chicken with a gigantic lorry before gleefully skidding out of the way at the last possible second.

Jimmy peeked through the gaps in his fingers to witness the car accelerating towards a speed bump at high speed. "Nooooo, it's not a ramp!" he wailed, too late, as the car hit the hump and launched high into the air. Time slowed down as the vehicle arched up and over, higher than the parked cars which lined the street. Jimmy saw a pigeon flap past his window and he held back the contents of his stomach as the car began to nosedive towards a taxi.

Grandma frantically spun the wheel, manically laughing at the boy's distress. "Whoooo, I haven't had this much fun since the sixties," she wailed as the car hit the ground, missing all obstacles by millimetres.

Seconds later, they were bouncing through the crowded marketplace. Stalls went flying up in the air, shoppers leapt for their lives and Grandma continued to laugh hysterically.

Mr Corset was still heralding his latest batch of stretchy knickers at five pounds a pair, as they burst through his underwear stall, taking half of the contents with them. Grandma turned her windscreen wipers to maximum but couldn't get rid of a pair of pink knickers that had hooked itself on and refused to budge.

How they'd managed to not kill anyone Jimmy hadn't the foggiest idea. He could barely watch the insanity that was happening all around him.

Before he knew it, they had screeched out of the other side of the market, zoomed past the post office and were in sight of the Twins' house. The old lady put her foot down once more, mounted the pavement and narrowly avoided a man and his dog who had wandered perilously close to the road. She slammed on the brakes, nearly launching Jimmy out of the front window.

They had arrived. The lad flung open his car door and projectile-vomited across the grass verge. He'd been on rollercoasters that had been far less traumatic than the ride he had just been on.

Once he had stopped quivering and shaking, Jimmy returned his focus to Ryan. He needed to get him into the house. He turned to grab his friend and was greeted with a grumble and a groan.

"What on earth happened? Why am I in Grandma's car?"

Chapter Seventeen

"It looks to me like this place is extremely well-guarded. I hope you're up to the challenge, Laila?" Jake grinned his usual cheeky grin as he passed her the binoculars.

From their viewpoint on the hill, it was clear to see the vast number of troops that patrolled the wall of the army barracks, and the subtle green glow that surrounded it.

"We are going to have to use every bit of stealth possible if we're going to get into there undetected," Jake added.

"Come on, Jake, use your head. All we need is a distraction. If we can draw the mutant soldiers out, then that gives us the perfect opportunity to sneak inside. Evil Dad isn't stupid enough to come out himself, but he'll happily send his zombified troops out to do his dirty work."

Laila threw the binoculars to one side and rooted around in her backpack. "And I know just the thing that'll do the trick." She pulled out a handful of the smoke grenades and timed paint bombs. "If we set these off near the woods over there, it should lure the soldiers outside the barracks. If I'm right they'll fall for it hook, line and sinker. Come on, Mr Speedy, you don't think I'm quick enough to run over there and back undetected, do you?"

"Right ok, ok leave it with me. Super Twin Jake will do all the hard work as usual!"

He dragged himself up off the grass, filled his pockets with the bombs and zoomed off towards the woods. Within a matter of seconds, a huge plume of smoke wafted out from the trees and Jake reclaimed his position on the grassy bank. "Was that quick enough for you?" he said, raising his right eyebrow. "There's only one Super Twin around here that has the skill and speed I have."

"Watch your head doesn't blow up too big, Jakey boy, or you'll give away our position. Now lie down, keep quiet and watch that gate like a hawk. When I say let's go, we move, and not a second before."

Jake was sure Laila was the one getting too big for her boots, but he did as she asked and waited patiently, holding his breath in anticipation.

As if by magic, the gates opened and out came one mutant, then another and another. Before long, a whole battalion had appeared, lined up in fighting formation. The troops marched straight towards the cloud that was blowing out from the undergrowth.

"See? What did I tell you?" Now's our opportunity. Come on, Jake, let's get in there now while we have a chance." Laila spoke with urgency as she ushered the twin up to his feet. "Let's go!"

Jake stooped low and sprinted for the entrance, Laila struggling to keep up behind him. They paused only once behind a ridge to check the coast was clear. Just as they approached the entrance, the barrier shot up and out marched an armed officer. Jake instinctively grabbed Laila and pulled her down behind a nearby boulder. "Watch out, you!" he hissed as another battalion marched out behind the leader. "We're going to have to be extremely careful here – those things look like they'd eat us alive."

When the last few remaining wolfmen had exited the base, he sensed their opportunity. "Right, now!"

Jake half-dragged Laila as they sprinted and rolled underneath the barrier just in the nick of time. He surveyed the inside of the base quickly and shimmied along the wall, leading his partner into a nook out of sight.

In a flash, Jake darted into a nearby guard post, quickly tied a pair of guards up and came out with a handful of uniforms. He chucked one over to Laila. "You'd better get this on and make sure your hair is tucked up in the hat. I'm not sure that multicoloured pigtails are part of military attire these days." Jake laughed as he pulled the oversized combat pants over the top of his Super

Twin suit.

"Right, cheeky, enough of your funny remarks," Laila retorted. "We need to find Evil Dad and end this."

"Hold your horses."

Jake stopped dead in his tracks and observed the base in action. This place was gearing up for battle, there was no question about it. Platoons and regiments marched past them, left, right and centre. There were hundreds of soldiers in there, if not thousands. The enormity of the task at hand dawned on Jake. Getting into the base was one thing, sneaking past this gruesome army and finding Evil Dad was another. This was going to require cunning, skill and a whole lot of luck.

He took a deep intake of breath and slowly breathed out. He blinked, wiped his eyes and looked again. At the far side of the yard was a particularly vicious-looking pack of half-wolf, half-human monstrosities and they were headed right towards them. "Don't look now but I think we've been spotted!"

It was at times like this when he really wished he had the brainpower of his brother.

Chapter Eighteen

"Jake's in danger; we have to do something!" Ryan strained to lift himself off the floral bedding, but the pain was immense.

"You're going nowhere, my dear. A cup of tea and lots of rest is the best medicine for you." Grandma mopped his brow with her trusty handkerchief and smiled her sweetest smile.

"But Grandma, I can sense it. I have to help him. You don't understand." He trembled as he spoke. Everything hurt; he was battered and bruised all over.

"I know more than you realise, my lad. We grandmas have a habit of finding out everything, you see. I was young once, too. You may think I'm a just an old granny but looks can be deceiving. I've done things in my life you couldn't possibly imagine. I've witnessed danger, excitement and seen things you wouldn't believe."

"You mean like completing a ten-thousand-piece jigsaw?" asked Jimmy, nearly falling off his stool as he doubled up laughing.

Grandma swivelled around in a rage. "Have a bit of respect, young man. If it wasn't for your cowardice, Ryan wouldn't be laid here right now, and you wouldn't be relying on ancient old lady to save your bacon. Now, make yourself useful and go and stick the kettle on. I can't think without a cup of tea."

As Jimmy sheepishly headed off to the kitchen, Grandma turned and gave Ryan a wink. She tottered over to the bed and stooped down close to him. "Ryan, I need you to trust me now. Close your eyes tightly and be as still as possible. This may hurt a little," she whispered in his ear.

Ryan felt his grandma's hands on his chest, gently pushing down; a warm feeling began to filter through his clothes. It was a warmth that quickly turned into a fire, which in turn became a furnace.

The heat began to spread across his body, the fire pumping from his heart, and through his veins. He struggled for breath as the flames inside him seemed to burn every cell in his body. The sweat poured off him, the pain was becoming unbearable. He couldn't take much more; he felt like his insides were boiling.

Suddenly, Grandma took away her hands and he blacked out completely.

***

Ryan opened his eyes and found Grandma staring back at him.

"Don't say a word to that little squirt, Jimmy.

You didn't think your old nan would have power too, did you?" She smiled a coy smile and Ryan noticed a twinkle in her eye. "Don't move too quickly but I think you'll find that your pain has eased somewhat."

Ryan began to stretch his arms out and found he had no pain left at all. Whatever his grandma had done had healed him completely. It was a miracle! How on earth had she managed it? And what else didn't he know about her? There were so many questions he needed answers to.

Grandma immediately interrupted his thoughts: "Right, my lovely. You told me that Jake's in danger. Where is he and what happened to him? Tell me everything – we're going after him, right now!"

Chapter Nineteen

They looked terrifying, even from a distance: packs of mutant wolves, marching on their hind legs. They needed to act fast – the creatures were rapidly approaching.

Jake turned to face Laila; he could see the fear in her eyes. "Don't look at them! Breathe and look natural. They might not have spotted us," he said.

But it was too late – the leader of the group, a huge beast twice the size of the others, was growling and motioning to the pack as they upped their pace towards Jake and Laila.

"They're coming straight for us!" Jake said without moving his lips as the pack of rabid animals broke into a canter.

Suddenly, there was huge explosion outside the base. A whole host of mutants came charging back in through the entrance, smashing right into the pack, some staggering, some limping, shouting and yelling. They were splattered with a rainbow of different colours – they'd walked right into Laila's trap. This was just the diversion they needed.

"Quick!" urged Laila. The pair shot off in the opposite direction to the commotion. They leapfrogged over a pile of pallets, barrel-rolled behind a parked truck, and then crept in between two containers.

"We need to get into that main building. It's definitely not safe out here with those wolf things on our case!" Laila struggled for breath as she spoke.

"You're telling me," said Jake. "The way that leader looked at me, it was like he wanted to devour me. I'll take my chances against Evil Dad instead, thank you very much. Come on, I'm not hanging about here."

The pair, as calmly as they could, slipped out from between the containers and strode across towards the main building in the barracks. Jake walked straight in through the door with Laila close behind him, both holding their breath as they brushed past rapidly moving soldiers. The place was a hive of activity; they'd have to be extremely careful not to be caught out.

Jake hadn't a clue where they were heading but kept his head down, pushing onwards through the maze of corridors and meeting rooms. More guards rushed past them as the corridor opened into a large open room. Beams of sunlight burst through a huge glass ceiling, illuminating the room. Shadows stretched across the floor, pointing to a passageway at the other side of the space.

"It has to be this way!" yelled Laila as she did a power slide across the floor.

Off they shot, zooming down the empty

passageway. This area of the base seemed completely deserted. Eventually they came to a door and cautiously opened it. Inside, they found an abandoned laboratory filled with vials, test tubes, beakers and flasks, strewn across workstations. A strange blue liquid in a pool on the floor caught their attention.

Click…

The door closed behind them. The pair swung round to see their old IT teacher, Professor Bios, standing in the doorway, a manic expression across his face.

"Ohh, look," rasped Bios. "If it isn't my favourite student, Master Jake. Have you come to take a look at my new place of work? It's a far cry from that sweaty little classroom, don't you think? Saying that, I couldn't have built this up without all the equipment I've stolen from school."

As he spoke, Professor Bios began to pace towards them. The glint off his orange-tinted glasses reminded Jake not to look into the Professor's eyes. This man was more dangerous than his looks suggested and they literally had their backs against the wall.

"I always knew there was something not right about you. You've been working with Evil Dad all along, haven't you?" Jake burst out.

"You mean our great dark lord? You could say we have been working together for a little while,"

Bios cackled. "He said you'd come to pay us a visit – we've been expecting you. I hadn't expected you in my lab quite as soon as you've managed it but let me give credit where credit is due. I never thought you were the brightest star in the constellation but even a genius like me can make the occasional minor miscalculation."

Jake bolted towards the man at warp speed, but the scientist had clearly anticipated this exact moment. He calmly slid a mask up around his mouth and smashed a large glass container of green liquid on the floor. The room immediately filled with a strange toxic gas. Jake and Laila instantly dropped like sacks of potatoes onto the floor.

Chapter Twenty

The engine roared as Grandma sped down the motorway, the engine of the car screaming out in pain and music blaring from the stereo.

Who was this person impersonating his grandma? Ryan thought. She'd gone from a tiny old lady with a penchant for tea and cake into a Superhero with healing powers. Here they both were, ready to perform the rescue mission of the century. Both he and Jimmy were clinging on for dear life as Grandma narrowly avoided several vehicles.

"Grandma, slow down! You're going to end up killing us before we have even arrived!" wailed Ryan.

"Oh, give it a rest, Ryan. Blame your little friend for calling me. If you ask for my help, then that's exactly what you'll get. Now keep your shirt on, we've got some bad guys to catch!"

The car bounced and groaned over bumps in the road as Grandma turned off the motorway, quickly heading into what looked like a farm. Driving straight across a field and splattering through cow poo, Grandma rammed through a mesh fence at the other side of the field. Much to the farmer's dismay, she then tore down an adjoining farm track, ignoring his angry cries for her to stop.

Suddenly, Ryan noticed a plume of thick black smoke billowing out from behind the car. "Grandma, the car's on fire!" he yelled over the din of the heavy metal music.

The car was indeed on fire and the flames were roaring from the rear of the car. Grandma quickly glanced in her rear-view mirror and smirked. "Right boys, on my count I want you to open your doors and jump…"

"Jump?! Are you crazy?" cried Ryan.

"Yes, absolutely completely and utterly bonkers. Now ready? 1… 2… JUMP!"

Without even taking a second to consider their options, the trio hurled themselves from the vehicle. The car zoomed off down the track by itself, colliding into an old stone wall.

BOOM!

The machine exploded into a ball of flames, the passenger door shot up into the air and landed in a nearby field, splattering cow poo everywhere.

"*That could have been me,*" thought Ryan.

"Well, I guess it couldn't handle my driving after all these years. Think I'll be better on the buses these days," laughed the old lady as she dusted herself off. "I never did like that car anyway. Are you boys alright?"

"Yeah, I think so – just a few bruises," replied Gold Shield. "Nothing that a trio of Superheroes can't handle," he said, puffing out his chest.

"This way!" called Grandma as she leapfrogged a nearby fence. "We're on foot from here onwards so get a move on."

The boys obediently followed behind her. It reminded Ryan of the country hikes that Dad used to take him on – there was never a moment's rest as they powered up hills and ran down streams. He remembered the time they got so lost they nearly had to call emergency services to rescue them. He recalled the look on his dad's face when Jake suggested calling for a pizza and making camp instead and the three of them ending up rolling around laughing on the floor. How things had changed since then.

"Come on, boys – concentrate. It's this way."

As Grandma powered on up and over a stile, Jimmy was puffing and panting trying to keep up with her.

Ryan tried to focus. They had to get to Jake and Laila before it was too late. They were in great danger and the Fast Food Festival was due to start soon. The Super Twins were the guests of honour.

The smell of fire filled Ryan's nostrils as they reached the woodland on the brow of the hill. They could see a plume of smoke in the distance, near the army barracks. They would have to be cautious now – they hadn't a clue what they would be facing. One false move could spell danger.

Ryan reached into his rucksack and pulled out a couple of butter guns. "Hey, Jimmy, catch," he called as he chucked one over to his teammate. "We need to watch our step now."

Grandma paused and sat down with her back against an enormous oak tree. She picked up an acorn and began to peel off bits of the outer casing. "Whatever is past that smoke isn't going to be a pretty sight. We're bound to be outnumbered so we need to be smart, stealthy and sly. We have to keep ourselves concealed and pick off one at a time." As she spoke she threw bits of the shell down onto the woodland floor.

Ryan and Jimmy crouched down in front of the old lady, hanging off her every word. They were ready for action, poised and alert.

"We need to be each other's eyes and ears. Especially ears, as far as you two are concerned, I can't hear just as well as I used to."

"What did you say?" quizzed Jimmy.

"Shut up, boy," she chuckled. "It's time to go."

The team readied themselves and began to advance forwards, hunched low to the ground. They trod carefully across the woodland floor, until Grandma stopped in her tracks, pointing down at the ground at the imprint of a boot.

"Fresh tracks," she whispered, before carefully

tiptoeing past the next tree.

The smog was getting thicker now, and it burnt Ryan's eyes. His heart began to pound hard in his chest, his mouth drier than a desert in the height of summer.

Snap!

A twig cracked in two, and to the boys' surprise, Grandma instantly cartwheeled off to one side as a small rabbit bounced off in sheer panic.

They continued onwards through the dense undergrowth, but eventually, through gaps in the trees, the trio could see the army barracks. They crept closer and crouched down low to observe the garrison.

Five minutes passed, then ten minutes. There was no movement at all. Another five minutes had passed when Jimmy said what they'd all been thinking:

"There's no one there, the base is deserted."

Chapter Twenty-One

The Fast Food Festival procession flowed right through the centre of Trincaster town centre. Banners hung from every window, balcony and strings of flags crisscrossed the square. A brass band belted out marching songs and the tuba player was so red in the face it looked like he would pass out at any second.

The Trincaster Fast Food Festival was the highlight of the year for the local residents. They consumed more junk food during that day than most towns produced in a year.

Floats featuring everything from the local burger-joint team, the pizza house and all-you-can eat-buffet flowed past. The crowd were cheering, waving and small children were screaming out with excitement. Around the sides of the town square, there were stalls selling candy floss, cakes, and a chance to play hook-a-duck. There was even a throw-slime-on-the-teacher booth.

The mayor was standing to one side of the stage outside the town hall, garbed in his official finery, checking his notes one last time before the opening ceremony. He adjusted his gold chains and shovelled down one last jumbo sausage roll while he prepared to make his entrance.

***

It was a sight to behold, a sight which absolutely disgusted Evil Dad as he watched from the rooftop of Quincey's bakery. Evil Dad studied the crowd with intent, watching his hooded mutants slip through the mass of people undetected. Everything was going exactly to plan.

As soon as the final floats disappeared through the square the crowds began to hush, anticipating the mayor's speech.

The mayor clambered up the rickety, makeshift steps to the stage and began to speak: "People of Trincaster, welcome to our famous Fast Food Festival, the ultimate party celebration dedicated to fried chicken, greasy burgers and doner kebabs."

The crowd cheered, waving a variety of unhealthy foods in the air.

"Today's festival also contains an extra-special element – a celebration of everyone's favourite local superheroes, the Super Twins."

The applause was deafening, echoing all around the square.

"We had planned to have the boys here to help unveil our brand-new tribute to them but unfortunately, they haven't arrived yet. They're probably tied up saving the world, or planning a dramatic entrance."

The crowd groaned and booed, many of whom

had come just to see the twins.

As the mayor droned on with the pleasantries of the day, the mutant army began to close in on the stage. Evil Dad watched as they encircled the mayor, who was oblivious to the growing danger.

This was his moment.

Evil Dad clipped himself to a harness and then to a wire that ran from the roof he occupied down to the side of the stage. In a flash, he zipped down the line before propelling himself onto the podium and grabbing the microphone from the shocked mayor. He hurled him out of the way to the side of the stage, kicking chunks of sausage-roll pastry that had dropped from the mayor's pockets.

"Speaking of dramatic entrances… I'm back!"

Chapter Twenty-Two

On seeing the return of the dark lord, the crowd went totally berserk. They began screaming, yelling and shouting at Evil Dad. Here they were, celebrating their beloved Fast Food Festival and the man who wanted to destroy all their unhealthy food had taken centre stage. This was their worst nightmare.

"Now, now, calm down people, the celebrations haven't even started," laughed Evil Dad. "We have so much to get through in such a short space of time. Compose yourselves. We haven't got close to the main event yet and you're getting over-excited. First things first, I've brought my very own special guests to the festivities. Mutants, show yourselves."

Right on cue, the army of wolfmen, dotted around the crowd, ripped back their hoods to reveal themselves. The people of Trincaster panicked and all set off in different directions, trying to escape, all with their own idea of the quickest route out of the square.

"Mutants, attack!" screamed Evil Dad.

This had the effect of stopping the crowd instantly in its tracks.

"Now come on, people of Trincaster, behave yourselves. They won't harm you if you do as you're told. We're building up to the part of the festival you've all been waiting for – the grand unveiling. It wouldn't be good manners to leave early before it gets started, would it?"

Evil Dad paced from one side of the stage to the other. "I hope you didn't mind me bringing along my lovely mutant friends to make sure you all take part in the festivities. It's all for your own benefit. I didn't want any of you to miss out on all the fun."

Evil Dad motioned to Gedeon to join him onstage. "I'd like to welcome to the stage the general of my newly formed mutant army, Gedeon. Give him a wave and a cheer, people. Gedeon is going to assist me in the grand unveiling ceremony, aren't you?"

The wolfman nodded, snarled, and marched across the stage to the huge covering that concealed the statue.

"Right, come on, Trincaster. I want you all to get involved." Evil Dad was laughing and cackling. "I'm going to countdown from five to one and when we get to one, you all cheer, okay?"

As he spoke, the mutants prodded and growled at the civilians in the square. They would obey him whether they liked it or not.

"5, 4, 3, 2, 1..."

Gedeon pulled the cord, the coverings dropped, and the crowd gasped. There, in front of them, was not the new statue but a gigantic lump of green, glowing meteorite. Next to it, in a small plastic prison cell, were the slumped bodies of Jake and Laila.

"Surprise!" laughed Evil Dad. "I bet you were expecting a statue of the Super Twins, weren't you? But instead, you've got the *real* Super Twins. Oh wait, one of them is a girl. Why don't you introduce yourself to the audience? Oh no, what a shame. She's knocked out from my chief scientists' formula and can't do that."

Jake attempted to retaliate: "You won gi away wiv thisss!" he slurred. "Wi nt finis yt!" As he spoke, he dribbled out of the corner of his mouth. The pool of drool soaked into his top as he tried to suck the remaining spit dangling from his chin back into his mouth.

"Still not got the feeling back in your face, boy?" Evil Dad laughed. "From where I'm standing, I can get away with just about anything I like and there is nothing you can do about it!"

This was all too easy for Evil Dad, and he was revelling in the glory.

Chapter Twenty-Three

It was far worse than Jake could possibly have imagined. Here he was, stuck in a plastic cage, barely able to speak, never mind move. All his strength had been sapped. Laila hadn't even regained consciousness.

Whatever Bios had used in that lab to knock them out was extra-strength; he wouldn't have been surprised if it contained cabbage or broccoli. Now all he could do was prop himself up and watch as events unfolded.

Evil Dad was starting to turn up the pace of the Festival. The brass band was increasing the speed of their music as he waved his arms erratically in the air. "Citizens, people of Trincaster, we are gathered here today to celebrate a new dawn in the town's history.

"Today we will celebrate not only the destruction of the Super Twins but also the rebirth of a place free from the distractions of fun, junk food and laziness. Trincaster will, under my leadership, become a beacon of hope for the future of this country; a town of hard-working, vegetable-eating individuals.

"But before this can take place, we need to destroy all of this town and start again. Out with the old and in with the new!"

With horror, Jake realised the crowd were hanging off Evil Dad's every word. The lump of meteorite was glowing bright and people were transfixed by it. They were falling under Evil Dad's control, turning into zombies, rooted to the spot.

Jake looked around the square at all the familiar faces in a trance, slaves to the dark lord who used to be his father. Why wasn't it affecting him or Laila? Perhaps the cage was protecting them from the glare of the meteorite, or maybe Evil Dad wanted him to view every bit of the show. Jake watched as he began to whip the crowd into a frenzy.

"Now it's time – time to destroy Trincaster!"

The crowd instantly went nuts. Stalls were overturned, banners ripped down, and cakes and chocolate sauce soared through the sky. The people who had spent so much time preparing for these celebrations were now destroying everything in sight. Jake was helpless to stop them. Where was his brother?

Evil Dad was waving his arms around with glee as he controlled the action. Chairs flew across the square, and people clambered over each other to destroy anything that wasn't already broken.

Just then there was an almighty crash and the whole crowd turned to look. Bursting into the square, running over everything in its path, was a gigantic tank. It screeched to a halt on the stage, smashing the glowing lump of meteorite off its podium. A hatch on the top of the tank opened up and out popped the head of Grandma.

Chapter Twenty-Four

Grandma, Gold Shield and Ryan jumped out of the tank one by one.

"You didn't think it would be that easy now, did you?" the old lady cried across the square. By dislodging the meteorite from the stage and knocking it out of sight, Grandma had helped the residents regain their senses. Evil Dad no longer had control of them and they were ready to fight back.

"Come on, everyone, let's take back our town!" yelled Ryan.

The people of Trincaster cheered and the place erupted into chaos. They charged at Evil Dad's creatures as pies, burgers and even the occasional chocolate bar were hurled across the square. Trincaster was uniting and nothing could stop them. Ryan witnessed one of the mutants being splatted in the face with a cream cake while someone from the kebab house battered him with a naan bread. Even the mayor had dived off the stage to get involved in the ruckus and was wildly swinging a deep-fried sausage around his head.

Just then, Ryan spotted Gedeon bursting through the crowd, running straight towards him. The Alliance of Superheroes jumped off the tank and down into the chaos below. Grandma set off towards Jake and Laila like a steam train, while Ryan's sights were firmly fixed on the mutant.

They clashed into each other, the wolfman's claws swinging wildly at the Super Twin. Ryan dodged and weaved out of the way. They traded blow for blow, until Ryan was knocked completely off course by the force of the beast charging into him. He plummeted straight down into the ground with a crash, feeling a searing pain down his righthand side.

Within a flash, the great bulky mass of Gedeon was pinning him down using his incredible strength, fangs bared, fur standing on end. "This is the end for you, it's well past my dinner time." He licked his lips and Ryan nearly passed out from the stench of the wolfman's breath.

Ryan snapped himself into action and threw Gedeon off him. He leapt up and power-punched the beast right in the stomach. Gedeon lurched off before lunging back towards the Super Twin. Ryan dodged, rolled and twisted – he had to finish Gedeon off before it was too late!

Ryan made a break, propelling himself out of danger, but Gedeon was far from finished, leaping high into the air and clamping onto the boy's foot with his powerful jaws. Ryan span out of control, smashing through a nearby donut stand. Gedeon leapt on top of him, biting his neck, his wolf claws digging into the twin's shoulders. It was too much for the boy and he began to pass out from the pain.

Then suddenly, the beast took a butter bomb to the snout and collapsed on top of him. Ryan couldn't believe his eyes: Evil Dad was dragging Gedeon away from him, his dark sunken eyes not deviating from the wolfman.

"I told you not to overstep the mark, general, so now you will pay the price for your actions." With that, Evil Dad tossed the creature far across the town square. Gedeon slumped down against the wall in a heap.

Evil Dad looked back over his shoulder at the boy as he ploughed back into the swarm of battling townspeople. Ryan was sure he saw a twinkle in his eye – something he hadn't seen for a long, long time.

Ryan raised himself to his elbows and found his brother, Grandma and Gold Shield had arrived to support him. He was hurt, but instantly felt better with them around him. Grandma had managed to break Jake out of the cage and had used her healing powers to revive him.

"I know he has some good still in him – he's still our dad. But we know he's being controlled by the aliens," Ryan croaked to his twin. "That meteorite has taken over his mind."

"He's no dad of mine," growled Jake under his breath. "You weren't captured and shoved in a cage like I have been. We need to finish him this time, once and for all. He's let us down far too many times."

Jake pulled his brother to his feet and they stood together once more as the Super Twins, staring their dad in the face from across the courtyard.

Evil Dad's eyes narrowed, his chest puffed up as he slammed his now-intensely glowing staff into the ground. "Get them, get them all!" he roared and the reaction was immediate.

Zombie soldiers and mutants streamed into the town square from every angle, a green glimmer emanating from the metal panel on their chest armour. They abseiled down walls, rolled in from alleyways and threw themselves at the gang.

The Super Twins and their team leapt into action, punching, kicking and throwing the dark army in all directions. Bodies flew left, right and centre. The more soldiers they took down, the more appeared.

Jake found himself face-to-face with a gigantic, particularly gruesome-looking guard who sported a patchy beard, a wonky eye and clearly hadn't discovered how to clean his teeth properly. The huge brute of a soldier rained punches down on the Super Twin, pushing him backwards. Jake grimaced hard, ducked from a flailing arm and launched one of his own power punches, sending the man tumbling into a swarm of mutants.

The team worked together, back-to-back, attempting to keep the mutants at bay, covering all angles. They seemed to be gaining the advantage, when Bios appeared out of nowhere and smashed a vial of another one of his lethal potions into the ground.

"Watch out!" yelled Jimmy the pack of wolfmen that had been under Gedeon's control charged through the green smoke. Gnashing, growling and snarling, they came bounding towards the Alliance.

Grandma launched a mutant high over the top of the group, knocking Bios over like a pin. It was another one down, but it was all becoming too much for the Alliance; there was only so long they could hold on.

Jake looked through the haze to see Evil Dad sneaking off behind the stage. "Ryan, we have to go after him! Come on, before he gets away again!" He waved his arm in the direction of the retreating super-villain.

Using all his concentration, Ryan sent a burst of his Super Seismic energy around him blasting the savage wolfmen back.

"We've got this now," shouted Gold Shield, as he began firing his butter-loaded machine gun at the beasts. The mutants slipped and slid all over the buttery floor. "You guys get after him! I'll cover you!"

The Super Twins nodded at each other. "Let's go!" they said in sync, and charged off in pursuit of Evil Dad.

Within seconds they had caught up to him – he hadn't got beyond the VIP tent. He swivelled around to face the boys, an evil smile across his face. He stood, arms opened wide, with the backdrop of the huge, green, glowing meteorite behind him. "This is the end for you two. My power is too much for you to handle." He breathed in a huge deep breath, absorbing the Auxen's energy.

"We'll never give up! Enough is enough. You have to be stopped! I know this isn't the real you. You can't let it control you," shouted Ryan at the dark lord who was once his father.

This sent Evil Dad into a rage. He thrust his staff forwards, sending a lightning bolt, the likes of which they had never seen before, straight at the twins. Ryan attempted to stop the force of his attack with his mind as his brother dodged to one side. Jake began to hurl anything he could lay his hands on at the villain, distracting him, while Ryan summoned all his power.

Evil Dad laughed hysterically as he swatted away the debris Jake was throwing with a swoosh of his staff. His power was incredible and they weren't strong enough to compete with him.

Jake climbed a nearby wall before dive-bombing the dark lord. At the same time, Ryan used every ounce of mental strength he had to compete with Evil Dad, but neither boy was a match for him. The energy he was absorbing from the meteorite was extraordinary.

Ryan felt his strength dwindling. He couldn't give any more than he already had.

"Your powers aren't even in the same league as mine!" Evil Dad's eyes narrowed menacingly, as his jaw tensed, his teeth grinding hard.

The green lightning bolt that emanated from the staff surrounded the boys. As they pushed away hard, their feet kept sliding back. Their power was fading – it was no use.

With their power, all hope was fading, Ryan began to lose consciousness…

It was all too much.

Chapter Twenty-Five

The boys looked at each other and knew exactly what to do. They were so much stronger together than they were apart. This was something they'd always known but at times were too stubborn to admit.

If only they had worked together all along, they wouldn't have been in this position, thought Ryan.

"You do remember I can hear your thoughts?" Jake smiled as their minds unified, forging the ultimate Super Twin connection.

They grabbed each other's hands and sent forth a Super Seismic Shockwave. It slowly pushed back the lightning bolt.

"Your power is nothing compared to the Auxen's. Even together, you don't even come close." Evil Dad was attempting to infiltrate the twins' minds.

The meteorite behind him glowed brighter than ever. The Auxens were completely controlling his mind and actions through the green rock. The aliens had altered him beyond recognition.

"Now's the time to destroy this planet, giving power to the Auxens. You will submit!" the dark lord yelled out.

The twins pushed back with every little drop of energy they had but they were being forced back again. It was no use, even their combined power wasn't enough.

"Yaaaaa!" Out of nowhere, Laila flew through the air and ferociously kicked the staff from Evil Dad's hands. She rolled, spun and aimed to punch him, narrowly missing. This was just the opportunity the boys needed…

"Laila, get out of the way!" yelled Jake, as she moved to one side.

The Super Twins fired their Super Seismic Shockwave hard at the dark lord, who was raised off the floor with the force of the blast and thrown back against the huge lump of meteorite.

"Who isn't strong enough now?" screamed Jake. "How could you do this to your own sons? We have to finish you this time, for the sake of everyone."

But the anger and hatred began to fade from Evil Dad's face as he looked at his boys. "This wasn't me, this was never me. My mind hasn't been my own, you have to believe me," he whimpered.

The Super Twins relaxed their grip, letting Evil Dad slide down the meteorite onto the ground. Kneeling on one knee, he looked up at the twins,

"I will always love you…" Then he lurched for his staff.

"Nooooooo!" yelled Laila.

Evil Dad grabbed the staff, swung around and drove it powerfully into the heart of the meteorite.

A thunderous noise nearly deafened the Alliance and the green glow was blinding. They shielded their eyes and were hurled across the stage as the force of an almighty explosion hit them.

***

Raindrops splattered against his cheeks as Ryan gathered his senses and looked up to see a dark and disturbing mass of clouds swirling above him. A crack of thunder erupted that was so loud, it made the windows of the buildings around them shake and rattle. The clouds glowed as bolts of lightning flashed across the sky. And then the heavens opened: the rain fell hard and fast, giant globules of water bouncing on the floor around them.

Ryan and Jake fell down onto their knees in relief. It was over – Evil Dad had destroyed the meteorite and in turn, the Auxen. He'd saved them from the aliens, but left so many questions unanswered.

Ryan felt Laila's presence as she put her arms around them both. "It wasn't your fault," she whispered. "You didn't have a choice." A tear ran down her cheek as she squeezed the boys.

They knelt there, watching the rain fill the huge crater in front of them. Ryan couldn't help but wonder what would have happened if things had been different.

As dark thoughts clouded his mind, Ryan looked up to see his grandma walking towards them, splashing through the ever-growing puddles.

"It never rains but it pours," said Grandma, as she gave the boys a massive cuddle.

And as they looked over her shoulder, Ryan was sure he spotted his dad disappearing down the alley by the takeaway and into the distance.

Chapter Twenty-Six

The tea pot made a glugging sound, the china cup tinkling as Grandma filled the last cup on the trolley and wheeled it into the lounge. "Tea and scones everybody?" she inquired, as she passed plates around the room.

"Only if you use clotted cream this time," laughed Jake.

"I don't know what you're talking about, young lad." She winked as she sniffed the jar of cream in front of her. "It's only a few days out of date – it's not going to kill you."

"It's not, but I might," giggled Laila as she jumped up and bashed Jake over the top of the head with a cushion.

"I suggest, children, that we all move back into our seats before I get involved," warned Grandma.

Laila backed off awkwardly and sat back down. She knew better than to push her luck any further.

"I think we've had more than our fair share of battles for one day, don't you? After all the excitement we need a bit of peace and quiet," Grandma said.

"I'm glad it's all over, but I'm sure going to miss our action-packed adventures," replied Jake.

"Something tells me we'll have many more adventures to come," laughed Ryan. "The meteorite may have been destroyed and the Auxen may be out of the picture for now, but where there is good there will always be evil. And unless my eyes were deceiving me, Evil Dad and Gedeon are still out there."

"I really hope for once you're wrong," taunted Jake. "I just want us to be regular Jake and Ryan for a little while."

Grandma smiled sweetly. "Who fancies a game of cards after we finish our scones?"

"Erm… we have homework to do, don't we Ryan?" Jake stuttered.

"Yeah, there is loads to do today!" He tried to hide his smirk as he avoided Grandma's glare.

"I think we all know you've done everyone's homework already, Ryan." Grandma looked at him inquisitively. "Besides I've never really liked cards. Heavy-metal music and ten-pin bowling are normally my gigs."

Jimmy, Laila and Grandma erupted into thunderous laughter. Ryan looked across the room at Jake's happy smiling face. Jake looked back and nodded knowingly at his brother.

In that moment, they realised that these were the people that were important to them; this was their family. They didn't have their mum or dad around them and that didn't matter. What they did have was a bunch of people that loved them, and that they loved too, unconditionally. They were one big team, and nothing would ever get in the way of that.

Have you enjoyed reading *The Super Twins two*?

Well then, why not leave a review at:

www.amazon.com

Without these reviews I wouldn't be able to pursue my hopes and dreams of becoming a full-time author and you definitely won't be reading *The Super Twins* sequel.

Obviously, I want you to be honest with your feedback; nobody likes a liar!

For more information and FREE content, you can find Andy and *The Super Twins* on:

www.andyslinger.com

www.facebook.com/andyslingeruk

www.instagram.com/andyslingeruk

https://twitter.com/andyslingeruk

About **Andy Slinger**

Andy is a 38-year-old single parent to identical twin boys Luke and Liam. Having spent most of his working life as a retail manager, he found that his real calling in life is writing children's stories.

He released the Amazon bestselling book *The Super Twins* in September 2020 to great acclaim and is working day and night to become a full-time author.

"My aim is simple: to **engage, inspire** and **entertain** kids with my stories."

For further information about Andy and for exclusive content, sign up for his newsletter at: www.andyslinger.com

Thank you so much for purchasing the first edition of *The Super Twins Two*.

As a special bonus just for you, please visit: www.andyslinger.com to download a free activity pack.

Printed in Great Britain
by Amazon